Find the Littlest Angels

as They Celebrate Christmas

Illustration, penciling, and front cover art by Dave Garbot

Illustration script development by Roger Brown

Copyright © 1993 Publications International, Ltd. All rights reserved. This book may not be reproduced or quoted in whole or in part by mimeograph or any other printed or electronic means, or for presentation on radio, television, videotape, or film without written permission from:

Louis Weber, C.E.O.
Publications International, Ltd.
7373 North Cicero Avenue
Lincolnwood, Illinois 60646

Permission is never granted for commercial purposes.

Manufactured in the U.S.A.

8 7 6 5 4 3 2 1

ISBN 0-7853-0328-6

Look & Find is a trademark of Publications International, Ltd.

PUBLICATIONS INTERNATIONAL, LTD.

Christmas is almost here, and there's a lot of work for us angels to do. But there's still plenty of fun to be had by all. Angels have gathered from near and far for our annual Cloud Sculpting Contest. My job is to make sure all the sculptors sign in. Can you find me, Grandma Angel, and then find these angels who are getting into the Christmas spirit?

Grandma Angel

Carol

Pippi

Precious

Clarence

Holly

Michael

Noelle

Merry Christmas!

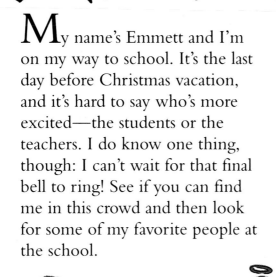

My name's Emmett and I'm on my way to school. It's the last day before Christmas vacation, and it's hard to say who's more excited—the students or the teachers. I do know one thing, though: I can't wait for that final bell to ring! See if you can find me in this crowd and then look for some of my favorite people at the school.

Emmett

Lacey

Music Teacher

Flight Instructor

Hall Monitor

Gabriel

Principal

Gym Teacher

The angels' greenhouse is always a busy place, but things really heat up at this time of year. Holly, mistletoe, Christmas trees—we have to work extra hard to meet the holiday demand. Give us a hand by finding these special Christmas gardening tools that we need to take care of our plants.

A wheelbarrow

Pruning shears

A spade

A trowel

A pitchfork

A hoe

Gardening gloves

A watering can

Hi, my name is Jack. Welcome to the Littlest Angel Christmas tree lighting ceremony. Everyone is here to join in, but we don't have all the ornaments. My job is to gather them up. Maybe you could help. Find me and then find all these missing ornaments.

Jack

A rocking horse ornament

A Santa ornament

A peace ornament

A bell ornament

An angel ornament

A star ornament

A little drummer boy ornament

It's almost Christmas and lots of people are wrapping and sending last-minute gifts and letters to loved ones. We have to work around the clock to keep up. Help us out by finding these special packages.

A piano

A toy train engine

A fishing pole

A ball and bat

A vase

A golf club

A television set

A bicycle

We're getting ready to put on a production of *The Nutcracker*. I never knew a Christmas play was so much work! The stagehands, the actors, the musicians, and everybody else are all working together, and we're having fun, too. My name is Lacey, and I'll be playing Marie, the star of the show. See if you can find me, and then find these other characters that appear in the story.

Marie

Fritz, Marie's brother

The Sugarplum Fairy

Uncle Drosselmeier

The Prince

The Dancing Flower

The Mouse King

The Nutcracker Doll

Bands, floats, balloons—isn't it great!! There's nothing like a parade for bringing people together, even on a cold day like today. Come join us, and see if you can find these bells that are ringing in the Christmas season.

Southern belle

Bluebells

Doorbell

Sleigh bells

Cowbell

Liberty bell

Tinker Bell

Silver bells

The North Pole is a busy place this time of year. This is Santa, and my angel friends have dropped by to help me get ready for my big trip on Christmas Eve. The gifts are all being wrapped and loaded, but a few of them have been misplaced. Can you find me and then find these gifts that haven't been wrapped yet?

Santa Claus

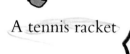

A necktie

A wagon

A tennis racket

A fire truck

A model airplane

A teddy bear

A doll

Family, friends, food, and fun! Christmas dinner has got to be the best meal of the year, even though it is a *lot* of work. See if you can find the chef angel and then find these special holiday treats she prepared.

Chef angel

Santa cookies

A pumpkin pie

Eggnog

Gingerbread cookies

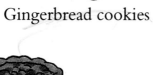

A mince pie

A fruitcake

Roasted chestnuts